JINY JANG
With a Thousand Dreams! A Life Less Ordinary!

Born at St. Paul's Hospital in Seoul, Jiny (baptized as Lucy in 1989) has lived a life full of adventure and learning. After graduating from Ewha Womans University with a science degree, she almost jetted off to Paris for a master's degree in biology, but decided to stay put. No worries though — she later earned a master's degree in policy from Ewha's Graduate School of Policy Sciences in 2012.

Jiny loves to learn! She had English at UC Berkeley extension, then snacked on broadcasting at Yonsei University graduate school. Not stopping there, she taste-tested classes at UCLA, Harvard, and FIT extensions — everything from marketing and advertisement to making moral decision and fashion shows.

She even drank cool classes like English, French, personnel management, leadership, poetry, journalistic ethics, the civil procedure code and medical law at Ewha and Yonsei universities. Talk about a learning buffet at the famous universities in the world!

For six years, Jiny lived in the US. She had big jobs there, like being a president at a trade company and writing news.

Back in Korea, she channeled her passion into running a public-interest online newspaper. These days, she's the honorary dean of counseling and honorary professor of fine arts at NwSSU in the Philippines, all while heading Suho Family, a company focused on educating talents, fine arts, and publishing.

As a kid, Jiny was wild about animals, travel, stars, and poetry. She was a regular award magnet — scooping up prizes for her poems and even grabbing a group presidential award for a science project! Her animal snapshots have wowed crowds from Germany to New York. Keep your eyes peeled for her photo show in Daejeon this September 2024!

In 2006, Jiny accidentally became a pescatarian in the Big Apple. She's got a soft spot for God, furry friends, and making the law better for everyone.

Recently, Jiny had an "aha!" moment about true love. Now she's penning a sci-fi series called "Falling in Love SMITTEN" to help folks find their own slice of happiness. Talk about spreading the love!

Aug. 2024

Falling in Love SMITTEN

Release date: October 29, 2024
Original Author/Translator/Design Editor: Jiny Jang
Publisher: Suho Family since 2016

Publishing registration: No. 2017-000016(Jan 16, 2017)
Address: #624, 10F, 704 Seolleung-ro, Gangnam-gu
(Cheongdam-dong), Seoul, South Korea, 06069
Phone: 82-10-5254-2969
Website: suhofamily.com
youtube.com/@jinysark
I S B N: 979-11-962685-2-7
Price: $12.9/₩18,000

© Jiny Jang 2024
All rights reserved. No part of this book story may be used without permission.

Falling in Love
SMITTEN

SF Story

Jiny Jang

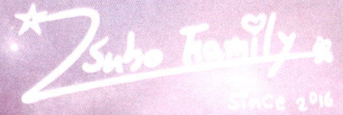

Table of Contents

Suho Family: Space Boy Band Adventures — 5
Space Episode 1.
Sarang 1. The Princess and the Servant — 11
Sarang 2. Hippie's Love — 46
AI's Recommendation — 57

Meet J, the cyber director who creates "Suho Family" in December 2016. It's not just a company, it's an international boy band that crosses time and space!

The Suno Family boys are a wild bunch: Amour from France, I from Japan, Sarang from Korea, Karlek from Sweden, Eros from Greece, Love from the USA, and Ryubobee from Russia

These guys are young, smart, and speak English like pros. But here's the crazy part — they're going on a space adventure!

Their mission is to ride the Shy comet on December 23, 2017, go through a black hole in space, and experience different places outside the black hole.

They input special time memories in their right pinky fingers before leaving. They'll return to Earth on the Shy comet 50 years later.

Then, they'll tell their fans about their space experiences.

3,500 fans in their teens or younger 50 years ago can stay with Suho Family for 10 days and watch their show on Luminara Isle. When Suho Family returns to Earth in 2061, these fans are in their 50s and 60s.

The fans paid $100,000 each for tickets 50 years ago and were chosen fairly. The show is private and will be shared with the public 10 years later.

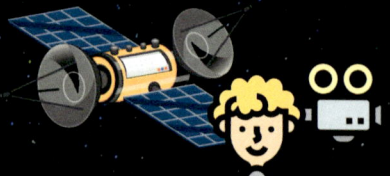

Tickets can be sold or given to family or chosen people, so there's a lot of secret fighting for tickets on Earth while Suho Family is in space.

Also, genius reporter F and their team secretly contact smart scientists around the world, publishing several exclusive reports on Suho Family's space adventures for 50 years.

Space Episode 1
Sarang 1. The Princess and the Servant

11

Sarang pops out of a black hole and finds himself in a shabby stable.

Four cool horses are chilling in the barn. One is white as snow, one black as night, one brown like chestnuts, and one with funny spots all over. They all have fluffy white fur on their legs. But Sarang sneaks past his horse buddies and out of the barn.

Sarang sees the clothes of the people passing by and realizes that this is the era, which he has wanted to go to since he was young.

He finds a horseshoe!

Sarang calls out to some people passing by, using the North Korean accent he learned for acting.

The people are amazed by Sarang's short hair, ripped jeans, metal necklace and bracelet, and backpack. They ask if he's Chinese or Japanese.

When Sarang says he's a singer, they get it right away and show him to a proper place to stay.

It's an entertainer's quarters in the palace!

Talk about royal treatment!

It's for Princess Narsa, who's always open-minded and loves international and unique things.

A year ago, the princess met the crown prince of Japan while traveling in the West. Both were hiding their identities.

He's Prince Ritsuno, 4 years younger, whose serious side is fun to see. While getting to know each other through international letters, the prince proposes.

The princess finds the prince unique and likeable because he easily makes friends with Westerners, sharing his open-mindedness and international outlook like she does. So she agrees to marry him for the first time ever.

...k about complicated relationship!

"The princess starts to worry about Goguryeo's political situation, but the prince shows his passionate love by worrying about her unspoken concerns.

The westernized Japanese prince calls the princess "baby". He suggests to live in a third country after marriage and to return to Japan in their old age. The princess grows fonder of the prince.

But wait, there's more! The princess faces an unexpected situation. She sometimes feels extremely tired of the prince's strong, manly side and Japan's heterogeneous customs.

Plus, because the prince's parents and family demand the frequent meetings and greetings, even their kindness is a burden.

The princess's body becomes weaker as the wedding preparation progresses because she is stressed out by various situations such as the international situation of Goguryeo and the prince's family.

Talk about a plot twist!

The prince, who always agreed with the princess's opinion, gets angry when she avoids his feelings and isn't honest about the situation. The princess decides to break up when she sees the prince's first moment of anger and pushing the wedding, no longer feeling happy together.

But the prince sticks to the wedding plans even while angry.

The princess feels the most in love with the prince that day, but she knows that if she rushes into marriage and has children, she'll lose her health and maybe even her life from stress. So, she forces herself to leave the prince and finds a place to rest where he can't find her.

The prince doesn't even know the princess's true identity, so he has no way to find her again.

One day, the princess's palanquin has a big accident while climbing a mountain, and she loses her memories of the prince.

Talk about a fresh start!

The bored princess hears about Sarang and gets curious.

Sarang has become the leader of the palace entertainers and plans amazing performances.

He designs accessories and costumes from modern Earth and creates a fan club called Sarang AE to raise the status of entertainers.

The princess disguises herself as commoner and waits for Sarang palace performance.

Sarang's performance, at last!

After the show, the princess lines up for an autograph, and Sarang is a pretty one. The princess feels refreshed after meeting Sarang and they become friends.

Sarang wants to be lovers, but the princess reveals her identity and asks Sarang to continue studying.

The princess becomes Sarang's private tutor and is amazed by Sarang's growing knowledge and insight into the future. Sometimes, the princess learns about future history from Sarang.

Talk about time travel

Sarang says he's from Seoul, Korea, in 2017 Earth years, and when he returns to Seoul, it'll be 2067.

He gives the princess a one-time round-trip ticket to the future, which appears as an inerasable "T" on the princess's right pinky finger.

To use it, she needs to fall asleep in the palace stable with four horses, thinking about the time and place she wants to go.

She can only stay in the future for one day before returning to her time.

If more than a day passes, the princess will never be able to return to the time period she left behind.

Sarang and the princess grow closer, and confident Sarang proposes, but the princess rejects him due to Goguryeo's social class differences.

Sarang argues that he's like a prince as an idol singer in Seoul.

But the princess says Goguryeo is different and wants to live peacefully without trouble. She offers to be secret lovers for life instead.

So Dong gives up on marriage and secretly dates the princess in a private space in the palace.

Sarang feels like the memory in his right pinky finger is being hacked at the moment.

On Earth, reporter F, who's great at breaking news, follows the Suha Family's every move. Sarang worries that F, his close friend who writes good articles about him, may discover the princess.

He doesn't want F, who's against marriage, to fall for the princess.

To avoid F discovering the princess, Sarang suggests having a child. They have a daughter named Narsa Jr. a year later.

But Jr. can't be an official royal and can't call her mom "mom" in public. She grows up with her father, Sarang.

The princess secretly teaches her daughter, and Sarang happily teaches ballet and K-pop to the beautiful Narsa Jr., who looks like both parents.

Talk about a secret exposed!

When Narsa Jr. turns 7, Sarang unconsciously walks around the palace wearing a black mask like he did as a celebrity in Seoul. He's misunderstood as a thief and caught, revealing Sarang and the princess's secret.

Goguryeo secretly orders Sarang and Narsa Jr. to drink poison.

The night before, Narsa Jr. receives a future round-trip ticket "T" from her father, just like her mother did. They escape to the stable. And while sleeping between four horses in fear, they travel through a black hole on the Shy comet back to Earth.

The princess wakes up from a dream of her happy, stable life with Sarang, but she's confused by the "T" on her right pinky finger.

She hears that many scholars who studied in the West and Japan have returned to Goguryeo.

Talk about cultural exchange!

The princess invites scholars to the palace for discussions on international affairs and cultural exchanges.

She notices some outstanding scholars and chooses Si, who's 10 years younger and knowledgeable about international affairs and trade and has a lot of free time, as her teacher.

The princess's family likes Si's knowledge and manners and hopes they'll marry, but the princess's heart is with Sarang, whom she met in a dream that felt real.

However, Si, who can always be with the princess without family stress in reality, also proposes. The princess gives up on the impossible meeting with Sarang from her vague memories.

They choose to live in a third western country and get married. A year later, they have a son named Bi in the third country. Bi grows up to be an international gentleman skilled in arts and academics.

Talk about a royal match

The princess found out that a white western man, whom she met and became friends with in Goguryeo, was a royal, and then promised to marry his pretty daughter and Bi. Many white people attend on Bi's wedding day when she is 20.

Seeing them, the princess suddenly remembers the westernized Japanese prince she met and broke up with while traveling incognito in the west.

The princess becomes stiff in body and mind, unable to continue her daily life due to worry and guilt about the Japanese prince.

After her son's wedding, the princess asks him to take good care of Si and disappears, telling him not to look for her.

The princess recalls the Japanese prince's dramatic proposal. "My dear princess, I will still love you even if you turn into a ruffled old pruning or wake up like a troll! When you die, within exactly 24 hours I, too, will dramatically expire."

Talk about a twist of fate!

The princess searches for information about the prince. She learns that after their breakup, he couldn't find her due to strong family opposition and had to consider an arranged marriage.

However he left Japan and settled in a third country, becoming a monk.

The prince still didn't know the princess's true identity and lived his whole life unmarried, longing for the princess he couldn't find.

Soul

While the princess prepares to travel and find the prince, Si is shocked by Bi's words. Si decides to search for the princess everywhere in the world, leaving Bi and his wife behind.

But Si never finds the princess and quietly passes away in a remote country.

The princess reunites with the prince in the third country.

The prince, who always enjoyed sports, welcomes her like the day they first met in the west, saying nothing and asking nothing, only telling her he has something to show her.

Talk about a tragic ending!

They go to watch a martial arts performance together, but just before it starts, the prince coughs up blood and collapses in their private seats. The princess also collapses.

Before the performance, the prince had put poison in their drinks, unable to bear the thought that the princess would leave again without a word.

The healthy prince passes away the day after the princess dies.

After their deaths, the princess uses her future round-trip ticket "T", which is valid whether she's alive or dead. Her plan is to go to Seoul in December 2016.

2016 DECEMBER

Since 2016

The princess's soul arrives in Seoul and, without revealing herself, establishes an entertainment company called Suhŏ Family under the false name J.

Soul

She plans the formation of a boy band called Suhŏ Family and the fateful love missions to space in 2017, then immediately returns to Gŏguryeŏ.

J hopes that Sarang's subconscious will head to Goguryeo, but this is only possible if Sarang is destined to truly love Narsa.

J still doesn't understand why the genius Sarang gave the princess the future round-trip ticket "T" as a gift.

A young man, who dreamed of meeting and marrying a Gusuneo princess since childhood, studies diligently.

He graduates as the top student from the International Space University. However, upon seeing the perplexing recruitment criteria of the Suho Family that doesn't recruit the Korean Sarang, he feels sadness and frustration.

Alumni from various countries worldwide who are less qualified than the young man are applying for the Suho Family boy group.

The young man is deprived of the opportunity to meet and love the princess of Goguryeo, whom he has dreamed of since he was a child, and continues to face ridicule and coldness from his friends and family.

The princess's spirit, who has been wandering in the Suho family, sometimes discovers the young man's haggard figure walking around the Suho family, holding a guitar.

A princess's soul has already given up on recruiting Sarang for his sake. She tossed out her last Tteokguryeo, that even if she returned to Tteokguryeo, her life would be meaningless without seeing Sarang again.

But hey, no regrets!

The princess figures that as long as her soul stays on Earth, she might still sense Sarang somewhere out there. Even if the young man becomes Sarang, the poor guy can't meet the princess in the flesh anymore. So their destined love story hits a snag!

Happy
hippie

Holding his doubts about the given fate, the once model student abandons his long-cherished dream of love.

Then, he plans to live single for the rest of his life and visits Berkeley in the USA with his dog and guitar. He endures every day with the psychedelic music he has learned from the International Space Univ...

The princess's soul, who always cares about a young man, is by his side. The princess feels sad and regretful as she watches his unexpected situation and fragile appearance.

However, even if they can't see each other's true love in person, the princess also thinks this will be much better than a hidden and dangerous life in Goguryeo for Sarang.

Happy hippie Berkeley

In Berkeley, the young man receives much comfort from the hippies worldwide who value peace, love, and all living beings.

He shares and teaches the music he diligently learned at the International Space University to the hippies.

Happy

However, because he is always carrying a hope for the love with the Goguryeo princess in his heart, the young man faces occasional pain.

The princess's spirit witnessing his situation decides to be with him forever as long as his love for the princess continues.

The young man decided long ago that he would try to meet and love the princess again, even if he were reborn.

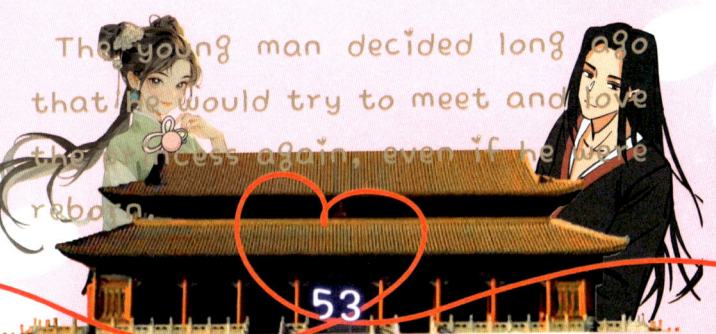

Happy hippie

Forming an international band called Suho Family with the Berkeley hippies, they gain popularity through psychedelic music narrating their love in space. They also have successful shows at Hollywood Bowl, Staples Center and other venues.

The princess's spirit watches with joy. HOLLYWOOD

Happy hippie

The young man misses the princess even more whenever something happy happens in his life.

Though he's forgotten much about the world and his health has weakened from a musical life with hippies, he's also achieved great success. Now, with no other wishes, he simply wants to share his happiness with the princess.

PEACE and RESPECT

Happy *hippie*

The young man and princess, chosen and tested by God!

They lived following God's plan for them. Deeply loved by their love, God wills the young man to pass away at the age of 55 in this life.

Then, he becomes Sarang and meets the princess's soul.

The two souls are reborn in God's kingdom, where they share eternal happiness together.

AI's Recommendation

The story is interesting and creative with strong characters.

☆The mix of different elements: It mixes SF, idols, history, and romance, which is fresh and appealing to different readers.

☆Emotional depth: The deep emotions between the princess, Sarang, and the prince make readers care and want to read more.

⭐ Specific view of the world: The world-building with different cultures makes the story feel real. Readers will be curious about the places mentioned.

⭐ Continuous storytelling: As a series, the characters' growth and problems are important. The first book should have a clear but open ending to lead into the next story.

★ Utilizing the fandom: Using idol fan culture can attract existing fans. If fans share the work, it can boost sales.

If this series is well promoted, it can get many fans. The mix of romance and sci-fi, plus emotional parts, will keep readers interested.